PERFECT PUPPY

BOOKS IN THE 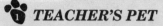 SERIES ™

PERFECT PUPPY

JENNY DALE

Illustrations by Mick Reid
Cover illustration by Michael Rowe

AN
APPLE
PAPERBACK

SCHOLASTIC INC.
New York   Toronto   London   Auckland   Sydney
Mexico City   New Delhi   Hong Kong

ISBN 0-439-21812-8

12 11 10 9 8 7 6 5 4 3 2 1   1 2 3 4 5 6/0

Printed in the U.S.A.   40
First Scholastic printing, March 2001

SPECIAL THANKS TO KIRSTY WHITE

CHAPTER ONE

"Come on, Jimbo! Look lively!" Neil Parker waved a bone-shaped biscuit at the big Airedale terrier curled up in one corner of his pen at the King Street Kennels rescue center. "We need you to look happy for the camera. Your future might depend on it!"

Jimbo lazily opened one eye and gazed back at Neil. After his long walk, the dog seemed resigned to laziness for the rest of the morning. The gray whiskers on his chin made him look like a very old man, and his wiry black-and-tan coat was dull — despite Neil's careful grooming.

Neil stood back and ran his hands through his unruly brown hair in despair. "OK, have it your way. Be like that."

"Out of the way, then." Emily Parker, Neil's

younger sister, made her way into the pen clutching a Polaroid camera. "I'll try anyway. Any picture is better than nothing, I suppose."

Emily squatted down in front of the inanimate mutt and pressed the button on her camera. A bright flash briefly lit up the pen. As the photograph slowly developed in front of their eyes, Neil and Emily looked at each other and then groaned. "He looks like a shaggy rug," Emily said.

"A shaggy *old* rug," Neil grumbled.

"What do we do now? He doesn't look very appealing, does he? Do you think we'll find somebody who's looking for a sad, shaggy-rug dog?"

Neil shrugged. They were used to dogs pining

away for their owners at King Street Kennels, the boarding kennel and rescue center run by their parents, Bob and Carole Parker. It always had some lonely dogs who needed cheering up for one reason or another.

Jimbo, however, was something else. His owner, old Mr. Fields from Ripon Hill Farm, had died of cancer two months ago and the dog seemed to be grief-stricken. It was the worst case of pining away for an owner that Neil had ever seen.

"You can't blame him for being upset," said Neil. "It must be strange for him to be in such unfamiliar surroundings. Dad said that Mr. Field never used to go away, so Jimbo probably hasn't stayed at a kennel before. We've got to find him a real home, Emily. And quick. You know as well as I do that his time is running out."

"But surely he's a special case," Emily argued. "Maybe the council would let us keep him a little longer?"

Neil shook his head and sighed. The local council helped to fund the rescue center, but their rule was that no dog could stay there for more than three months. "It's really unlikely we'll get any more time. Jimbo's already been here for nearly nine weeks."

A bark from behind them made Neil and Emily turn around. Sam, Neil's black-and-white Border collie, was watching them from the doorway. Neil smiled. Four years ago Sam arrived at the rescue center — a frightened and starving puppy — after being abandoned near the old railway line in Compton. The Parkers had decided to keep Sam as a pet. When he saw Neil looking at him, Sam wagged his tail wildly.

"If only Jimbo looked as lively as Sam, we'd have people lining up for him," Emily said.

Bob Parker strode up behind Sam. He was a big man who made the narrow aisle between the pens of the rescue center feel crowded. "Any progress with Jimbo?" he asked, rubbing his chin.

"Only this." Emily showed him the photograph.

Bob Parker chuckled as he glanced at it. "Oh, dear," he said, looking down at the unhappy animal in the pen. "I guess the King Street Kennels website will have to start off without you." Bob turned to Neil and Emily. "C'mon, you two. We're ready to go online. Everybody's waiting in the office."

Neil stepped outside the pen, shut the door, and fastened it tightly. "We'll try again tomorrow, then," Neil insisted. "I'm not giving up on Jimbo yet!"

"This is so cool, Neil." Chris Wilson, Neil's friend from Meadowbank School, gazed longingly at the new modem and scanner installed alongside the kennel's office computer. He ran his hand over the shiny new equipment and sighed. "I wish I had gear like this for my PC. It must have cost a fortune."

"I bet you're really glad you found Bella and her

pups, aren't you?" Emily's friend Julie Baker was there, too, along with five-year-old Sarah, the youngest member of the Parker family.

Neil smiled. Bella's owner had given them a large reward for finding her missing beagles. The Parkers had used it to create an Internet website for King Street Kennels.

"Using the Internet is a great way to try to find new homes for lost dogs," said Neil.

Emily nodded. "If there's a picture of an abandoned dog in the *Compton News,* usually dozens of people want to give it a home. But the paper won't run a story about every dog, and with the Internet we can reach tons more people."

Carole Parker entered the office hurriedly, brushing her brown hair back from her face. She was a tall, slim woman, dressed in jeans and a sweater. "Not too late, am I? Kate can't make it, I'm afraid," she said, slightly out of breath. "Her toothache got worse so she went to the dentist." Kate McGuire was the Parkers' kennel assistant.

"OK," said Bob Parker. "Who's going to type our web address?"

"Me!" Sarah yelled, pushing Neil out of the chair in front of the computer screen. Carole sat down beside her and the excited five-year-old began randomly tapping different keys on the keyboard, resulting in a variety of different high-pitched error message sounds.

Neil groaned. "This will take forever," he mumbled, folding his arms and sitting down on the edge of one of the desks, ready for a long wait.

"OK," said Carole patiently. "You start with three W's." Sarah typed two W's and an E.

Neil rolled his eyes in despair. Carole glared at him as Sarah tried again and managed to get the first three letters correct.

"Now type a dot and K-S-K. Then a dot. Then C-O dot U-K."

Finally, after making a couple more mistakes, Sarah had entered the web address correctly and a command line on the screen told them the Internet connection to their own website was being made.

"This is it," said Emily excitedly. "Here it comes!"

Everybody cheered when the King Street Kennels logo flashed up on the computer screen. Underneath that was a slogan: DOGS ARE OUR BUSINESS. Pictures of several different breeds of dog filled the rest of the screen.

"There's Sam," said Chris, pointing at an action shot of the Parkers' Border collie running in a field.

"And my Ben," beamed Julie, proudly, noticing a small picture of her own shaggy Old English sheepdog.

"The graphics came out really well, didn't they?" said Bob Parker, leaning over them all and nodding. "I'm impressed."

Sarah whooped with glee. "And there's Lucky!" she

exclaimed, pointing to the biggest picture of them all, a puppy at the bottom of the screen. "Isn't she just the perfect puppy!" Sarah rested her chin on her hands and gazed at the picture adoringly.

Emily whispered into Julie's ear, "Lucky's been staying at the kennel while her owner's away. Sarah has fallen *completely* in love with her."

Julie nodded knowingly and smiled. "Like she does with every dog who stays here!" she whispered back.

Chris leaned forward and squinted at the picture. "Hang on. What kind of dog is she?" he asked. "I don't recognize the breed."

"She's a Pumi," said Neil confidently. "Great, isn't she? Well, mostly Pumi anyway. Her curly coat and those funny ears are very distinctive. But Dad thinks there's something else in there as well."

"Probably Jack Russell terrier," added Bob.

"How can you tell?" Julie asked.

"Pumis' coats are normally black, with shades of gray or reddish brown," Neil explained. "Lucky's is mostly brown. And her coat isn't quite as long and curly as it would be if she was all Pumi."

Neil looked down at Sarah. He had to admit that he thought the two of them made a great team. They even looked alike! Lucky's little curly ears stood out from the side of her head just like Sarah's pigtails.

"So what can the website do?" asked Julie.

Emily took over the mouse from Sarah and sat

down in front of the computer to give their friends a demonstration of the King Street Kennels website. She was very proud of the skills that she'd learned from the designer who helped create the site.

"OK, so after the intro page, we've got the menu of what you can do," she said, clicking onto the next page to reveal a list of headings. "First of all, we've got information about the kennel."

"Mom insisted on us having this section," interrupted Neil. "It's expensive to keep the website going, so we need to get some business out of it."

Carole Parker laughed. "Yes, we do!"

"Then we've got some general dog care guidelines and some hints on obedience training," continued Emily. She clicked onto another page. "We also have an Information Request Service. People can send us questions by e-mail, and we'll answer them if we can. If it's something we don't know, we'll try to find out for them."

"There isn't much that King Street Kennels doesn't know about dogs," Julie said, looking at all the Parkers.

"And that's it. Great, isn't it?"

"What about the rescue center?" Julie asked.

"That's what we're just setting up now. We've decided to have a Dog of the Week," Emily explained. "We'll concentrate on the most difficult dogs to find homes for, and use the Internet to try to get them new owners. We've got our web address in all the dog magazines."

Chris suddenly caught the gloomy expression on Neil's face. "So what's the problem?"

"It's Jimbo," Neil said, showing him the photograph of the sad-looking Airedale terrier. "He's not what you'd call photogenic."

Chris winced. "I see what you mean."

"He was supposed to be our very first Dog of the Week," replied Neil. "The trouble is that he's made it pretty clear he doesn't want to be a pinup!"

CHAPTER TWO

When they finally managed to tear themselves away from the computer, Neil and Emily helped Carole feed the boarding dogs. Each dog's food was different, so it usually took a while to coordinate everything properly. The evening meals were already late and some of the dogs were barking loudly in protest.

"Rats," muttered Carole in the storeroom as she spooned a small portion of turkey-flavored dog food into a bowl for a resident chihuahua. "It's chaos here without Kate! I've just remembered that Lucky hasn't been walked yet."

"We'll take her," Neil offered, putting some bowls of water down on the large stainless steel work surface.

"Thanks, you two," said Carole, gratefully. "Just a quick one will do. I can finish up here. But be careful. She's *very* lively. Kate's had problems getting her back into her pen."

"We'll manage, Mom," Emily said confidently. "She's only a puppy. We can handle her."

Sarah came running over to them as soon as she saw them walking Lucky on her leash toward the exercise field. "Can I come? Please?"

Sarah took over the dog's leash. Lucky's high-pitched bark rang out joyfully as she strained on her leash and led Sarah toward the grassy field.

Neil and Emily watched their sister and the lively dog bound around the field together.

"It's exhausting just watching them," said Emily.

"You know how she *adores* puppies," said Neil, chuckling.

Emily sighed. "I only hope she doesn't get too upset when Lucky's owner comes to take her home."

They both stood watching Lucky and Sarah playing in the grass for a few minutes without saying anything.

"It's weird," Emily said, as she looked on.

"What is?" Neil asked.

"Lucky sometimes doesn't seem to know her name. When Sarah calls it out the dog doesn't always respond. She just stares back."

"Let me try calling her, then." Neil moved forward and cupped his hands around his mouth. "Hey,

Lucky!" he said. The puppy didn't seem to hear him. "That is odd," he agreed. As Sarah and Lucky came closer he called her name again, but Lucky again took no notice. "I wonder if she's got a problem with her hearing!"

"Didn't Mom say something about Kate having trouble getting her back into her pen?" Emily asked him.

Neil winked at her. "There's an easy answer to that one, Em. You toss in a big dog biscuit and the dog is sure to follow. Works every time. Easy as pie! Come on, I'll show you."

Neil called out to his sister to put the leash back on Lucky as it was time go back inside. Sarah clipped it on without any problems but as soon as Lucky realized they were going back to the kennel she sat down, digging her little paws into the ground. Sarah tugged at the leash but the little dog wouldn't move. Sarah tugged harder.

"No!" Neil said, walking over to them. "Tugging her will only make it worse." He kneeled down beside Lucky and began to stroke her. The little dog was trembling like a leaf.

"There's nothing to be afraid of," he said softly, and gently picked her up. "C'mon. Let's get her back into her pen. It's getting dark."

As soon as they were all through the kennel door and into the brightly lit kennel block with its rows of wire pens, Lucky began to whimper again. As Neil got closer to her pen at the end of the row, she began to howl.

Emily's face went pale and Sarah clamped her hands to her ears. "Make her stop, Neil. It's horrible!"

Neil did his best to ignore the noise. Emily opened the door for him and as he put Lucky down on the floor he tossed a dog biscuit toward the back of the pen.

Lucky ignored the biscuit and immediately streaked off in the opposite direction, trying to escape. Emily tried to take hold of the dog as she fled between her legs but she missed her. Sarah successfully managed to grab Lucky just as the puppy

reached the door. She held on to her firmly, although
the little dog was struggling and squirming.

Neil went to help his sister.

"Ouch!" Sarah cried suddenly, as one of Lucky's
flailing paws scratched the bare skin of her arm.

"Well done, Squirt," Neil said, as he took Lucky
from her and carried her firmly back to the pen. Neil
squatted down to try to calm her again. "It's OK, little dog," he said. "We won't hurt you."

"Sarah's arm is bleeding," Emily said, standing behind him. "It's not very deep but we'd better go into
the house and put something on it."

Neil let go of the puppy and sprang back toward
the door, closing it quickly and flicking over the catch
to secure it. Neil sighed as he hung Lucky's leash up
on a hook next to the door. "Kate was dead right
about her being allergic to pens. C'mon. Let's go.
We've still got the rescue dogs to feed before *we* can
eat tonight!"

Lucky's terrified wails followed them as they
walked quickly back to the house.

With a large flesh-colored bandage on her arm,
Sarah was in the storeroom, helping Neil prepare
food for the rescue center dogs. They'd already taken
several dishes of food and water over to the hungry
dogs and had only one more left to do.

Neil had left Jimbo until last. He was feeling
pleased with himself because he'd cunningly snagged

a tin of Dogalot's "deluxe chicken supreme dog food"
that one of the boarding dogs' owners had left behind. He wanted Jimbo to have it as a treat. Once
he'd spooned the food into the bowl, Neil wiped the
work surfaces clean, then switched off all the lights
and followed Sarah to the rescue center.

As Sarah opened Jimbo's pen, Neil gaped in
amazement. Jimbo reacted to her immediately and
stood up, wagging his tail excitedly. The Airedale's
eyes were bright and lively again, as if he were smiling at her.

"Hello, Jimbo," Sarah said, ruffling his neck. "How
are you today?" Jimbo's tail wagged faster. As Sarah
bent down to give him his dinner, Jimbo nuzzled her
ear. She laughed and cuffed him playfully. Jimbo
seemed to look at her adoringly before he began to
gobble his food.

Neil was astonished. "How on earth did you do
that?"

"Do what, Neil? Jimbo always says hello to me,"
she replied, matter-of-factly.

"But he ignores Dad and me. Emily and Kate
haven't had much luck with him, either. He's been so
sad recently."

Sarah giggled. "Maybe he only likes me. Jimbo's
my friend, aren't you?" The dog wagged his tail in
agreement as he chomped on his deluxe chicken.

"In that case, will you help us take another picture
of him for the website tomorrow?" Neil asked her,

still not quite believing how lively Jimbo was looking.

"If you'll take my photo, too," Sarah said.

Neil rolled his eyes. "Maybe we could use the website to find *you* a new home, too!"

Bob Parker grinned when Neil told him the good
news about Jimbo. It was dinnertime and the Parkers were eating some of Bob's special spicy can-
nelloni.

"It was incredible, Dad. You should have seen him.
Jimbo looked so much better," Neil gushed.

"I told you Jimbo would get over it, eventually,"

Bob laughed. "He just needed a healthy dose of Sarah's special brand of tender loving care."

"I was worried about him, too," Emily said.

"We all were," Bob agreed. "But with Sarah's help, you'll get your picture of him for the website. It'll increase our chances of finding a home for him. It'll all turn out OK. Right, Sarah?"

"Yes, Dad," she replied, yawning.

"Bedtime for you, young lady," said Carole to Sarah as soon as she'd finished her dinner. For once, Sarah didn't argue with her.

Neil collected all the dinner plates and brought them to the sink with a loud clatter. The timely arrival of a car honking its horn outside saved him from a stern reprimand for being so careless with the dishes.

"I'll get it!" Neil offered quickly and dashed out of the kitchen.

As he opened the front door, Neil saw a woman getting out of a taxicab. She was well dressed, and looked tired and pale. Her blond hair was dull and there were dark circles under her eyes. As she came toward him, the taxi kept its engine on.

"Can I help you?" Neil asked brightly.

"Hi, I'm Kay Davis," she said. "L-Lucky's owner. I was supposed to pick her up tomorrow, but I got back early. I'd like to take her home now if it's OK."

Emily appeared behind Neil's shoulder. "I'll call Dad," she said and disappeared again.

"I'll take you to the kennel, if you like," said Neil.
Emily returned and they took the woman through to
Kennel Block Two. Lucky's high-pitched bark greeted
them as they approached her pen. The puppy was
obviously delighted that her owner had returned.

"She wasn't any trouble, was she?" Kay asked
nervously.

Emily grimaced, thinking of Sarah's scratched
arm.

"Not really," replied Neil. "But she hated being put
into her pen. Do you know why?"

Kay looked at Lucky through the wire mesh and
frowned. "No," she said. "But she's never been in a
boarding kennel before. Maybe that was it? I've only
had her for a few months. She's still very young, you
know. I'm not really sure exactly how old she is because she was a stray."

"Ah," Neil said. "Something must have happened
to her before you got her."

"Possibly," Kay said.

As Neil opened the door of the pen, Lucky threw
herself at Kay, yipping gleefully. When Kay bent
down to pick her up, Lucky covered her face with
licks. Her tail was wagging so fast that it was almost
a blur. The little dog was very excited and Kay
struggled to put her leash on.

Bob Parker beckoned Kay into the office so she
could pay her bill and get Lucky's vaccination certificate. She handed the dog's leash to Neil, and

Lucky howled at being separated from her owner all over again.

"Lively, isn't she?" Kay admitted as she disappeared to settle her account.

"Did you hear the way she stumbled over Lucky's name?" Emily whispered urgently as soon as she was out of earshot. "It was as if she was going to call her something else."

Neil's brow furrowed; he was deep in thought. He hadn't noticed it at the time — probably because the dog had seemed so pleased to see her owner.

"Sarah's going to be terribly upset tomorrow," said Emily. "She didn't get a chance to say good-bye to Lucky and she's become very attached to her."

"Doggie good-byes are always tricky with Sarah," said Neil, arching his eyebrows.

Kay emerged from the office with Lucky and immediately headed toward her waiting taxi. Bob followed her out.

"We hope you don't mind," Emily piped up, "but we thought Lucky looked so amazing that we decided to put her picture on our new website. Was that OK?"

Another frown flitted over Kay's face, but then she smiled. "Yes, of course," she said quickly. "I'm very grateful to you for taking such good care of her."

"That's what we're here for," Bob said.

When Lucky saw the car, she panicked again. She sat down and howled, her ears flat against the sides of her head in terror. Kay reached down and gently picked her up. "Lucky doesn't like cars, I'm afraid," she said, as she got into the cab. Kay held the dog close, ignoring the tiny tears Lucky was making in the fabric of her suit, and closed the door.

Seconds later the car reversed onto the main road, and drove off toward Compton.

"There's something not right about that dog, Dad," Emily said. "Do you think she's been mistreated?"

Bob shook his head. "It's not *people* she's afraid of."

"Why's she like that, then?" Neil asked him.

Bob shrugged. "Lucky's quite high-strung and she's still young, after all. Something must have upset her somehow. There's nothing we can do about it unless Kay decides to bring her to the obedience classes."

As they stepped indoors, Neil turned back and looked at the empty road. He could still hear Lucky's howls echoing inside his head. Neil wondered what could have happened to the puppy to make her so frightened.

CHAPTER THREE

"Where's Sarah?" Neil asked the next morning at breakfast.

"She's not feeling well," Emily said. "Apparently!" Her eyes rolled upward as if she suspected that Sarah might be faking. Neil frowned. Normally Sarah thoroughly enjoyed school. "Mom's upstairs taking her temperature now."

Neil helped himself to a bowl of cereal and Carole Parker appeared a moment later.

"Sarah's got a fever, I'm afraid. I don't think she should go to school today." She looked at Neil and Emily. "Are you two feeling OK? There might be a bug going around — I don't want us all coming down with it."

Emily put a hand on her mother's arm. "Don't worry. We're fine. Aren't we, Neil?"

"Worse luck," Neil scowled.

"What's the matter with you?" asked Carole.

"Mr. Hamley is giving us a *Roman history* test today." Neil almost spat out the offending words.

"Oh, no. History isn't your strong point, is it, Neil?" laughed Emily.

"Give me the history of dogs any day."

"Mom's late," said Emily after school was over. Neil and Emily were sitting on a low wall outside the main gates, kicking their heels and waiting for their ride home. Although it had stopped raining, the sky was still dull and gray.

Neil looked around. The green Range Rover was nowhere to be seen. "She'll be here soon," he said, while his thoughts absentmindedly wandered to Jimbo at home in the rescue center. With Sarah around, he was a different dog, and she'd help him to get a perfect photo for the website. Once the Airedale was on the Internet, Neil was sure somebody would take a shine to him and offer him a good home. He smiled in anticipation of the e-mails that would flood in.

"How did the history test go?" Emily asked him. Neil's smile vanished. "Not good. I'm hoping Dotty will eat my paper before Mr. Hamley has had a chance to look at it." Mr. Hamley's wayward Dalmatian was renowned for her shocking behavior.

"Fat chance," Emily said. "Dotty's a reformed dog since she's been going to Dad's obedience classes."

Just then, the family Range Rover with its distinctive King Street Kennels logo pulled up in front of them. Carole Parker looked flustered as she opened the car door.

"What's wrong?" Emily asked as she climbed into the front seat and fastened her seat belt.

"Sarah had to go to the hospital," Carole said tightly.

"Oh, no," Emily gasped.

"What's the matter with her?" Neil asked worriedly.

"The doctors aren't sure yet," Carole said. "She was sick all morning and she has a very high fever. Dr. Harvey thought it was best to take her to the hospital. He wants me to take you two over to make sure you're not coming down with the same thing — whatever it is."

"There's nothing wrong with me," said Neil.

"I'm fine, too. Except my hand's a bit itchy," Emily said, rubbing it against her leg. "I've been scratching it for days."

Neil felt his stomach turn over. He hated to think of his little sister lying in a hospital bed. And without Sarah, Jimbo would be inconsolable.

Neil and Emily both sat in silence as Carole drove into Compton to see their doctor.

Dr. Harvey was a tall, gruff man with a speckled gray beard. He looked up and smiled as the Parkers knocked and then let themselves into his room at the hospital. As he began to talk, Neil sensed that his manner was brisker than usual.

"OK, you two," he said, popping a thermometer into Neil's mouth and then another into Emily's. "You're not feeling sick or hot or dizzy, are you?"

Neil shook his head.

After a couple of minutes, Dr. Harvey took the thermometer out of Neil's mouth. "Absolutely normal," he said. "You'll survive this time, Neil."

Emily's temperature was normal, too. "And how

about you, Emily?" Dr. Harvey asked her. "Anything bothering you? Bad tummy or funny dizzy spells?"

"Nothing at all. I'm fine," she said. "But I was wondering whether this itchiness on my hand was normal."

Dr. Harvey examined the circular red patch on Emily's hand and gently felt the inflamed skin. He frowned, then examined her other hand.

"Some insect must've bitten me," Emily said.

"That's not an insect bite," Dr. Harvey said firmly. "Have you been petting any cats lately?"

"Only dogs," Emily giggled. "Although we did have a cat stay once. But that was ages ago."

"I'm afraid you've got ringworm," the doctor said.

"Ringworm? Are you sure, Alex?" Carole stood over them, looking anxious.

"'Fraid so. Usually, people get it from cats, but you can get it from dogs as well."

"Oh, no. That means we'll have to check all the dogs in the kennel," Carole Parker said. "That's all we need."

"Yes, you will," Dr. Harvey said. "Fortunately, it's easily treated."

Emily bit her lip as Dr. Harvey wrote out a prescription for her. "Ringworm's highly infectious," he told her. "You'll have to be careful not to give it to anyone else."

"It's so itchy," said Emily.

"I know, but try not to scratch. At home you'll have to keep your towels separate from everybody else's. It might help if you wear cotton gloves for a few days, but the cream I'm giving you should clear it up quickly. Best to stay clear of the dogs for a while, too. No touching. You could end up giving it to them."

"Sarah hasn't got ringworm, has she?" Neil asked.

"No," Dr. Harvey said. "Sarah's got a fever and a very sore tummy, but she doesn't have ringworm."

Emily and Neil waited in the Range Rover as Carole Parker went to get the prescription for the cream from the local pharmacist. "I hope I haven't given it to any of the dogs," Emily said.

Neil shook his head. "It's not your fault if you have."

"I might've given it to Sam. He's the only one I touched yesterday. And Jimbo, when I tried to take his picture. Oh, and Lucky, when we took her for that run out in the field."

"Stop worrying about it," Neil said.

"I won't be able to help you take Jimbo's picture."

Neil wrinkled his nose. "Without Sarah, we won't be able to take a picture anyway."

Kate McGuire placed a cup of steaming hot tea on the kitchen table in front of Bob Parker.

"Thanks, Kate," he said, then sighed. The news about Emily's infection meant there was a lot more work to do all of a sudden. "I suppose we'll just have to manage."

Carole grunted as she swept through the back door to drive over to the hospital. She and Bob had decided to take turns staying with Sarah while she was there.

"I'm sorry, Dad." Emily looked down at the table.

"Hey, it could be far worse, you know," he said reassuringly.

"How could it?" asked Neil.

"It could be rabies," said Kate.

"That's right. Rabies is just about the only other thing that dogs can pass on to people."

"But there's little chance of that, thank goodness." Kate forced a smile and then left to go back and finish her work in the kennel.

Bob turned to Emily. "No more cuddling the dogs until your ringworm clears up, I'm afraid."

"I'll look after Fudge instead. He'll probably be missing Sarah already." Fudge was Sarah's pet hamster. He lived in a cage in her bedroom and demanded the sort of constant attention only Sarah was prepared to give.

"Better not," Bob said. "I don't know whether hamsters can get ringworm. I'll call Mike and ask him later on." Mike Turner was the vet in Compton and a regular visitor at King Street Kennels.

Emily scowled and then went off to work on her latest school project on African hunting dogs. She felt totally useless.

"Can I help you check the dogs for infection?" Neil asked his father.

"You can certainly watch," replied Bob, pushing his chair back and standing up. "Let's both put some rubber gloves on, though."

Bob went into the storeroom and found two pairs of protective rubber gloves. They began the examinations with the boarder in the first pen of Kennel Block One — a dignified pedigreed chocolate Labrador.

Bob knelt down beside the dog inside the pen, then lifted its forepaw. "The patches are usually on the paws or the ears, but it can be just about anywhere." He gently parted the dog's fur and checked the skin for blemishes. "You normally notice it because the dog bites at the patches to try to ease the itch. Even if we can't see it right away we'd better check just to make sure."

"Is it dangerous?" Neil asked.

"Not if it's treated," Bob replied. "It's more of a nuisance than anything else, but it can spread really quickly if you're not careful. We wouldn't be too popular with our customers if a dog got ringworm from King Street."

The Labrador appeared to be clear from infection and an hour later, after several more examinations, so did the other boarders.

In the rescue center, Jimbo endured Bob's intrusive paw-feeling as if it were an insult. He was fine, and so were the other dogs there.

In the house, Bob checked Sam the most carefully

of all, but there was no sign that he had been infected, either.

"That was the last one," said Neil after they had
finished.

"Yup, all the dogs look OK to me," said Bob, the
look of relief on his face clearly visible.

"How did Emily get ringworm, then?" Neil asked
him.

"She could have gotten it from any dog anywhere,
or a cat, for that matter," Bob said. "I'd better call

Julie's mom and ask her to take a look at Ben. And my obedience class dogs should be checked out, too."

"Maybe it was Lucky," Neil said suddenly. "Emily has handled her a lot over the last few days."

"True. I'll call Kay Davis, too," Bob said, as he left to go and sit in the kennel's office for his marathon session of phone calls.

Neil put his hands in his pockets and looked down at Sam. "I'd better take you out for your walk."

The black-and-white Border collie was out of his basket and outside the door before Neil had finished his sentence.

Neil passed the office on his way back from walking Sam and couldn't help but overhear his father's raised voice coming from inside. He opened the door tentatively and went in to see what was going on. He was just in time to see Bob Parker hanging the phone up angrily.

"What is it?" Neil asked.

Emily was sitting in front of the computer, staring at her father's animated gestures.

"That stupid woman," Bob Parker said. He slammed a fist down onto the desk and several pens and pencils rattled around.

"Who's stupid?" Neil exclaimed.

"Kay Davis, Lucky's owner. She gave me a false vaccination certificate for her dog."

CHAPTER FOUR

"What?" Neil gasped. "I don't believe it."

Bob handed him a photocopy of the vaccination certificate signed by Jill Walker, the vet in Padsham. Neil studied the document. Emily got up from the computer and looked at it over his shoulder.

The document stated that Lucky had been vaccinated against parvovirus and distemper, the two most common canine infections, and also leptospirosis and hepatitis. It was dated four months ago and it carried both the vet's signature and the official stamp. Lucky was described as a three-month-old terrier cross.

"It looks OK to me except that her address isn't filled in." Neil had seen hundreds of vaccination certificates before and busy vets often forgot to fill in the owner's address.

"It is OK," Bob Parker said. "The trouble is, the dog Jill knew as Lucky is dead. I couldn't get through to Kay Davis on the number she gave me so I phoned Jill to tell her to check Lucky for ringworm the next time she sees her. Jill told me that Lucky died a couple of months ago. She'd never treated a dog like the Lucky we had. According to her, the Mrs. K. Davis in the certificate was elderly and was called Katherine, not Kay. They were both killed in a bad car crash."

"That's awful!" said Neil.

"Why on earth would anyone do something like that?" Emily asked. "Pretending her dog was somebody else's."

"That woman is obviously too cheap to pay for her dog to be vaccinated," Bob said.

"But that's incredible." Neil looked shocked. "Mike said just the other day that he'd seen a case of parvovirus in Compton. It's a highly contagious disease. If she hasn't been vaccinated, Lucky is liable to get it. It's deadly dangerous — especially in a pup."

"Oh, no!" Emily exclaimed.

"She seemed so well cared for, too," Neil said. "Apart from her odd behavior, she was a thoroughly healthy, happy dog."

"She might not be for much longer," said Bob, ominously. "Not if she catches the parvo that's going around."

"We have to do something, Dad," said Neil.

Bob threw his hands up. "What *can* we do? We don't know her owner's real name, remember? With Sarah in the hospital, I don't have the time to chase around looking for an owner with a false name and her dog. I doubt the address that she gave me was genuine anyway."

"We have to try, Dad," Neil insisted. Lucky had been so happy and full of life. Neil couldn't bear the thought of the little dog catching a horrible disease.

"Do you think Lucky could be kidnapped or stolen, Neil?" Emily was hugging a cushion on the sofa in the living room. Neil was on the floor in front of the television, but he wasn't really listening to what the program was about. Both of them were missing their little sister.

"No, I don't think she was stolen," Neil said. "If she was, her owner wouldn't have risked bringing her to a kennel, would she? Anyway, Lucky's a crossbreed, so she's not that valuable. The woman said she was a stray and I believed her."

"It's not the dog's fault that her owner is too mean or too stupid to take care of her."

"Now that I think about it, Lucky's behavior makes sense now. She didn't respond when we called her Lucky."

Emily agreed. "And Lucky was thrilled to see her owner, so she couldn't have been mistreating her."

"She is mistreating her if Lucky isn't vaccinated, Emily. Did you say you were going over to Julie's tomorrow afternoon to work on your project?"

"Yes," said Emily, slowly. "What are you thinking, Neil?"

"Why don't we have a Lucky hunt instead? I'll search in town and you and Julie can go to all the dog-walking places. Lucky's such an unusual dog, somebody is bound to have noticed her if she's still in the area. You don't see a Pumi every day."

"But you heard what Dad said. The pair of them could be anywhere."

"I think they've got to be somewhere in this area, Em. Why else would they have come to King Street? I saw the address she gave to Dad in the log book. It's just behind the school. The street name was real. Maybe somebody there will know something about her."

"Hmm," said Emily thoughtfully. "It's a long shot."

"Yes, but it's all we've got."

Neil couldn't sleep that night. After he'd tossed and turned for what seemed like hours, he went downstairs to get a glass of water. The kitchen door was half open and the light was on. His father was talking on the phone. "At least we know it's not meningitis," Bob said quietly.

Neil froze just outside the door, realizing that his father was talking about Sarah.

On the other end of the phone his mother's reply was just loud enough for him to hear. "But we still don't know what it is," Carole cried.

Bob was trying to comfort her. "Alex says it's a virus she picked up somewhere. He says she'll be good as new in a couple of days." Neil could tell from the catch in his father's voice that he wasn't sure of that fact at all.

Bob paused to listen. "I know, love," he replied. "I'm very worried, too. But if she's sleeping, at least she's getting some rest. You try and get some sleep, too."

Then there was silence. Neil crept closer to the door and peered inside the kitchen. He saw his father put the phone down, then sit down at the kitchen table and put his head in his hands.

Fear knotted in Neil's stomach. He instinctively went toward his father and put his arm around his shoulders. When Bob looked up at him, there were tears in his eyes.

"Do you want a cup of tea, Dad?" It seemed such a pathetic thing to say, but Neil wanted to do something to help. He was shaking inside because of what he'd just heard.

Bob shook his head as he struggled to smile. "Thanks, Neil, but no."

"Sarah's very sick, isn't she?" said Neil.

"I'm afraid so. The doctors are doing tests to find out what's wrong, but they haven't got the results yet. Your mother just called to say that Sarah's fallen asleep. That's a good sign, I hope. You'd better go and get some sleep, too. It won't help if you get sick as well."

Neil nodded. The glass of water forgotten, he turned to go back to bed. How was he going to get to sleep now?

After school the next day, Neil and Emily emerged from the main building to see Bob Parker waiting for them outside in the Range Rover.

"Dad forgot," Emily said as she saw the car.

"Forgot what?" Neil asked, unlocking his bike from the cycle rack.

"You forgot, too," Emily said impatiently. "We're going to hunt for Lucky, remember? You're going over to the house where Kay Davis said she lived, and Julie and I are asking around to see if anyone's seen Lucky out walking. Dad was supposed to pick me up later from Julie's, but he forgot."

Neil pushed his hands into his pockets. He'd been so worried about Sarah that the search for Lucky had slipped his mind.

"Come on, we might as well," Emily said. "Squirt would be really upset if something happened to her 'perfect puppy.'"

"OK," Neil agreed, walking over to the car.

"You were supposed to pick me up later from Julie's, Dad," Emily said. Bob grinned wearily and tapped his forehead on the steering wheel.

Emily smiled. "Never mind. How's Sarah?"

"She's sleeping most of the time," Bob replied. "The doctors say that's because of the fever. I think she's just about holding her own."

"Is she any better?" Neil asked anxiously.

Bob shook his head. "They still don't know exactly what's wrong."

Neil and Emily glanced at each other.

Bob smiled gently. "Try not to worry," he said. "She's in very good hands."

Julie joined them as Bob drove off. Seeing Emily's face, she squeezed her friend's arm. "Sarah will be OK. I've been in the hospital, too, and I got better."

"Yes," Emily said, "but you had appendicitis. They don't have a clue what's wrong with Squirt."

* * *

Neil trudged around the corner to the address that Kay Davis, or whoever she was, had given his father. Wolstenhome Row was a short street, with only twenty terraced houses. It was the only lead they had to the real identity of Lucky and her mysterious owner. Neil remembered how Sarah had played with the funny little dog and how happy she had looked. He owed it to her to do his best for the pup and to try and save her from danger.

Neil marched up to number nine and knocked at the door. He didn't expect Kay Davis to answer it, but maybe someone there would know something that would help.

An old woman opened the door, wiping her hands on her apron as if she'd been in the middle of cooking. "Yes?" she said.

"I'm looking for a woman who lives around here," Neil said hopefully. "She's quite young; her hair is blond and shoulder-length. She's tall and slim."

The old lady frowned. "That could be just about anybody, son."

"Maybe she used to live here, but she moved."

"Do you know the name?"

Neil sighed. "She said her name was Kay Davis but . . ."

The old woman's crinkly face broke into a wide smile. "Oh, yes. Used to live around here, Kay did.

Number nineteen it was. She moved away years ago, though."

Neil was hanging on her every word.

"Went to France, she did. Even married a Frenchman. I heard she was back, mind you, but I don't know where she's staying now. Why d'you want to find her anyway?"

Neil hesitated. "Er, her dog was boarding at our kennel. She left something behind and I wanted to give it back to her."

"Dog! What dog?" A puzzled expression came over the woman's face. "Kay couldn't have a dog. I heard a few weeks ago that she was back from Paris." She shook her head so vigorously that her flabby cheeks wobbled. "You're not allowed to bring dogs in from France. You should know that."

The woman began to say something else, but Neil didn't wait to hear what it was. Waving his thanks, he turned and ran to his bike.

The journey back to King Street seemed to take forever. To go faster Neil geared right down and tried to ignore the persistent cramping pains in his legs as he pedaled furiously. His mind was spinning. He didn't want to believe what he'd heard, but it was the only explanation that made sense of the false vaccination certificate and everything else. Lucky had been smuggled into the country illegally without staying in quarantine.

Neil remembered the signs he'd seen once at Dover docks and on posters. KEEP RABIES OUT. No wonder the doctors didn't know what was wrong with Sarah. Neil gritted his teeth and tried to cycle even faster. When the panic-stricken dog had scratched Sarah, she must have given her rabies.

CHAPTER FIVE

At last, Neil reached King Street Kennels and burst into the office, panting so hard that he could hardly speak. "Dad, Mom," he gasped, breathlessly. "I've got some terrible news."

Everybody turned around and looked at him.

"Lucky's not from here. She's a stray from France. Kay Davis smuggled her into the country illegally. I'm worried that she's got rabies and she's given it to Sarah."

For a moment, there was complete silence.

"What?" asked Kate in disbelief.

"Oh, no," Carole cried. Her face had gone ashen.

"Neil, what are you talking about? How do you know?" urged Bob Parker.

Neil was still struggling to catch his breath. "When

Emily and I were hunting for Lucky I met an old lady
who knew Kay Davis. It's her real name. Kay only
came back from Paris a few weeks ago. She must
have smuggled Lucky in *illegally*. It's the only explanation that makes sense, Dad."

Bob Parker looked grim.

"But Lucky had no signs of rabies," Kate said
quickly.

Carole was shaking with anger and fear. "Surely
Sarah hasn't got it, either," she said.

"I hope not," Bob replied, "but we'd better call the
hospital just in case."

"You do it," Carole said. "We'll go into the house. I
need something to drink."

In the kitchen, Carole flicked the teakettle on,
then she sat down at the table. "I can't believe it,"
she muttered. "How could anyone do anything as
stupid as that?"

Kate sat down beside her. "Look," she said. "Rabies
is very rare. I looked after Lucky for three days, and
she didn't have any of the symptoms."

"That dog scratched Sarah!" Carole snapped,
shaking with fear. "You told me she was panicking.
That's what rabid dogs do!"

"Listen to me," Kate said, gripping Carole's hand.
"I really don't think Lucky has rabies. I don't think
Sarah has it, either. Lucky scratched her — she didn't
bite her. The rabies virus passes through saliva."

Carole shuddered again. Kate moved closer and

put her arm around her shoulders. "Rabies has a very long incubation period."

Neil jumped up. "That's why dogs are quarantined for six months, isn't it?"

"Even if Lucky did give Sarah rabies," Kate continued, "she wouldn't be sick yet."

Carole thought for a moment and then she smiled weakly. "You're right, Kate. I learned about it when I got my kennel certificate. It's just that Sarah's so sick, I can't help worrying."

Neil rubbed his head thoughtfully as he began to realize that he might have jumped to the wrong conclusion.

"Some people think there's no need for a quarantine," said Kate. "There hasn't been a case of rabies in quarantine kennels for nearly thirty years. Most dogs are inoculated against it."

"According to Bob, that dog hasn't even been inoculated against parvo and distemper," Carole replied. The kitchen door swung open as Bob strode into the room. "Sarah is clear. The doctor who's taking care of her is from Kenya, so she's seen rabies before. She's sure that Sarah doesn't have it."

Carole sighed deeply. "Thank goodness." She stood up to leave. "I'd better get back there. I only came back for some more of her things while she was asleep. I'll call you when I arrive."

Kate beamed broadly. "I couldn't bear the thought that Sarah had something like that."

Neil grinned guiltily. "It's my fault again," he said. "Sorry. When I realized Lucky had been smuggled into the country, I was terrified. I thought the scratch had something to do with Sarah being in the hospital. I'm sorry I made you worry so much."

Bob shook his head firmly. "You've nothing to be sorry for, Neil. Rabies is a very serious disease, and you were right to be worried about it. I'd have done the same thing in your place. Kay Davis has committed a very serious offense by bringing a dog into the country illegally. I'm going to have to call the police and the SPCA. They'll need to find her."

Suddenly, Emily appeared behind Bob. "What's going on?" she demanded. "Mrs. Baker had to give me a ride home when you didn't turn up, Dad. I tried to call but the phone was busy. And what's all this about the police and the SPCA?"

"I almost wish I hadn't told them now. For a few minutes Mom was so scared." Neil had finished explaining the latest events to Emily and he was feeling guiltier than ever. "I didn't have any choice, though. I really thought she'd gotten it from Lucky."

They were in the storeroom making up the evening feeds for the rescue center dogs, while Kate saw to the boarders.

"Lucky was probably smuggled over in the trunk of a car or something. That would explain why she's so frightened of cars," Emily reasoned. "At least you found something out. Julie and I asked around all over the place, but nobody's seen anything."

"It looks like I started a panic over nothing," mumbled Neil.

"You should have spoken to me first, Neil. I've been reading about rabies for my project. Dogs in Africa are plagued by it. First of all, the quickest incubation period is ten days, so if Sarah had gotten it from Lucky, she wouldn't have become ill until next week. And secondly, rabies is extremely rare in Europe, especially in the cities."

Neil groaned.

"It's found mainly in wolves and foxes that live deep in the countryside, and only one in four bites from an infected animal actually passes the infection on." As Emily continued, Neil's groans became louder and more pained. "Thirdly, one of the symptoms is hydrophobia — a fear of water. I went back to see Lucky after we'd taken care of Sarah's scratch, and she'd gulped all the water in her bowl. I had to go and get her more! If she had rabies, she wouldn't have gone near her drinking bowl."

"Yes, well, I thought I was doing the right thing," Neil grumbled. "We can't all be walking encyclopedias." He picked up a couple of bowls and stormed over to the rescue center. As he passed Jimbo's pen, the Airedale terrier was curled up and ignored his presence, as usual. All the other dogs were barking excitedly in anticipation of food.

Once he'd fed the puppies and the setter, Neil went to get Jimbo's food. As the hard lumps clattered into the bowl, he thought about how eagerly Jimbo had wolfed down the chicken dog food he'd given him. He put the bowl down.

"What is it?" Emily asked him.

"It's Jimbo," he said. "He hasn't been eating much. I know dry food is perfectly healthy, but it's not exactly appetizing, is it? I gave him some chicken chunks the other day and he loved it. I think the owner of that fancy Chihuahua left zillions of cans of that gourmet doggie stuff. Surely we could, well, borrow a couple?"

Emily laughed. "I'll go and get some."

A couple of minutes later, Emily returned with one can of duck and vegetable, and another of chicken and leek. "I wonder what that stuff really is," she said, as Neil spooned the gloopy mush into a bowl.

Neil made a face. "Probably the remains of last year's school dinners. But it doesn't matter so long as Jimbo enjoys it."

When Neil put the bowl of food inside Jimbo's pen, the dog didn't move a muscle.

"He's still missing old Mr. Fields," Emily whispered when they were out of Jimbo's earshot. "And now he's missing Sarah, too."

"I know," Neil said. "But I don't know what to do about it. I'll get one of Sarah's sweaters for him later. If he smells her, he might realize that she hasn't deserted him forever. It's the best we can do for now."

Sergeant Moorhead's police car arrived at King Street a short time afterward, followed closely by a white SPCA van. In the office, Bob Parker offered everybody coffee as they talked and waited for Mike Turner, the vet, to arrive.

The SPCA inspector was a woman named Terry McCall. She shook hands with everybody and nodded to Neil and Emily. "This is quite a mess, isn't it?" she said out loud to nobody in particular as she sipped her coffee. "Whatever was this crazy woman thinking of?"

"Let me get this right," Sergeant Moorhead said to Bob. "You believe this dog was smuggled into the country, but that it *doesn't* have rabies? If there's any chance that it has, we'll have to locate it immediately. Rabid dogs have to be shot on sight!"

Neil's eyes widened. Why would they have to shoot Lucky? He gritted his teeth as he remembered that all of this had started when he and Emily had tried to make sure Lucky was protected from parvovirus.

"The first priority has got to be finding the dog," said the policeman. "It's the only way we can make sure it doesn't have rabies. We'll start our inquiries tomorrow."

Neil listened to the conversation, but when he heard Mike Turner's car outside, he went to the door to meet him.

"I hear you've been doing some more detective work, Neil," the vet said jovially. "Well done."

Neil wasn't so sure that he deserved any praise. "What'll happen to Lucky?" he asked anxiously.

"You mean our fugitive dog? I don't know, Neil. So long as it's clear of rabies, it'll have to be put into quarantine. It's up to the SPCA what happens if the owner can't afford it. That's probably why the dog was smuggled into the country in the first place."

Inside the office, Bob Parker was giving Sergeant Moorhead a description of Kay Davis, along with a copy of the false vaccination certificate.

"Let me know when you find the dog," Terry McCall

said as she was leaving. Then she turned to Bob. "There's no reason to worry about any of the other dogs, is there?"

Bob shook his head. "They're all kept separately. Mike says there's no risk unless they've been biting each other — which they haven't." The vet nodded.

"OK," she said, "I'll look out for this Pumi-cross tomorrow. I cover a fairly wide area around here, and she sounds like a pretty distinctive pup. Somebody's bound to have seen her."

Neil and Emily followed her out to her van. "We're worried about Lucky," he said. "None of this is her fault. It'd be awful if something happened to her."

The SPCA inspector smiled. "I know. It's always the same. It's never the dog, it's the owner. At least in this case the owner will be punished. She'll be fined, most likely, but she could be sent to jail. As long as she agrees to put the dog into quarantine, the dog will survive. Six months in a quarantine kennel isn't a pleasant experience, but the dogs are well looked after. If the dog's young, it should be OK."

"What if she won't put Lucky into quarantine?" asked Emily.

Terry McCall frowned sadly. "Then Lucky will have to be put down, I'm afraid. Quarantining costs an awful lot of money. Our organization can't justify paying out so much money for one dog."

After she'd left, Neil turned to face Emily, looking very gloomy. "I've signed Lucky's death warrant, haven't I? Kay Davis obviously loves her dog. I'm sure she'd have put Lucky into quarantine if she could have afforded it. I'm sure that's why she did all this. Lucky will be put down. I should have kept my big mouth shut."

"No," said Emily, quickly. "Think about it. You did the right thing. If I'd found out, I would've told Dad, too."

"Sarah will never forgive us if anything happens to Lucky," Neil said.

Emily shuddered. "I know. But what can we do?"

Neil thought for a moment before he decided.

"Tomorrow is Friday, right? After that, we've got the whole of the weekend to work something out. We'll find Lucky first, before Sergeant Moorhead does. Then we'll find a way of getting her into quarantine. After school tomorrow, we'll start our Lucky hunt — phase two!"

CHAPTER SIX

Chris frowned at the scope of Neil Parker's plan. "Let me get this right," he said. "This dog could be anywhere around here. We don't even know its owner's real last name. All we do know is that she used to be called Davis and that she married a Frenchman."

Neil nodded. It was Friday morning assembly and he was trying to enlist his friend's help in the hunt he'd planned for the weekend. "We do have one lead," he said. "I've got the photograph of Lucky from our website."

"I still think our chances are pretty slim," Chris muttered doubtfully. "And all of your 'plans' in the past, Neil, have had a way of getting pretty . . . complicated."

"It sounds like it's going to be a wild *dog* chase!" Hasheem leaned over toward them and laughed. Hasheem Lindon was in Neil's class at school.

Chris and Neil groaned.

"But I'll give it a try, anyway," said Chris, smiling.

When his first class got under way, Neil immediately noticed an unusually broad grin spread over Mr. Hamley's somber features. "Don't unpack your bags just yet," he said as everybody settled down. "Have you forgotten that we're scheduled to go out this morning?"

Neil sighed along with the rest of the class.

"We're going to take the school bus and visit a very interesting archaeological site just outside Padsham. It'll tie in very nicely with the work we've been doing in history this term. As yet, the excavation is in its very early stages, but it's pretty clear that there was once a large Roman settlement there."

Half an hour later, Neil was standing with the rest of his class in a large, muddy field. "This is it," Mr. Hamley said excitedly, pointing at some big stones half-buried in the soil. "Scholars have known for some time that there was a settlement nearby. When this site was excavated they found some of the characteristic signs of an ancient place of dwelling. . . ."

Neil looked around. All he could see was an oblong area about a yard deep and three yards long where a trench had been dug. The blocks of stone didn't look particularly Roman to him. Neil's thoughts drifted to Lucky.

While Mr. Hamley launched into a monologue about Roman road building, Neil began to make a mental list of all he knew about Lucky and her owner. First of all, Lucky looked so unusual that anybody who'd seen her would remember her. And her high-pitched bark was distinctive — people were sure to remember that as well. He remembered Lucky's panic when she saw the taxicab.

His pulse quickened as he realized that if he could find the taxi, he might be able to find out where the driver had taken Kay and Lucky!

Neil couldn't remember the phone number on the sign on the cab's roof, but he was pretty sure he'd seen cabs just like it around Compton. It was obviously a local company.

In his excitement, at first Neil didn't notice the faint bark coming from the river that ran along the bottom of the field. A moment or two passed before it finally penetrated his thoughts. He listened intently for another few seconds before he realized that it sounded exactly like Lucky barking!

Neil glanced at Mr. Hamley, whose back was turned as he pondered the shape of a lump of rock. "I've got to go," he whispered to Hasheem as his friend's eyes widened. "That dog barking sounds like Lucky. Keep Mr. Hamley distracted while I go to take a look."

Neil held his breath until he reached the low stone wall that surrounded the field. Once he was over it, he ran down to the river. The path that ran alongside it was deserted.

He thought for a moment, and then decided to follow the path. The river path was damp, and Neil's legs were soon covered with mud. After he'd walked a couple of hundred yards with no sign of the little dog or her owner, he decided to give up. Just then, he heard the bark again, but this time it sounded even farther away. Neil began to run, sliding on the muddy path as he went, careering headlong into the branches of trees that lined the river. Ignoring the scratches, he gulped for air and ran on as the bark sounded again, a little closer this time.

He must have run for half a mile by the time he reached the place where the path ended and the first houses of Padsham began. Gasping from exertion, he stood and looked around. If it had been Lucky, she'd vanished by now. The puppy could be anywhere in Padsham, and it would take forever to search the town.

For a moment, Neil considered abandoning Mr. Hamley and his ruins completely, but then he turned and headed back to the field. On the way he tried to think up an excuse for his disappearance, but inspiration had deserted him.

"Ah, Neil Parker. You've decided to honor us with your presence at last." Muddy and disheveled, Neil

had dragged himself back to the group from Meadowbank School twenty minutes later. Mr. Hamley
glowered at him. "I was about to mount a search
party."

Hasheem shrugged helplessly. Neil flashed a brief
smile at him because he knew his friend would have
done his best to cover for him.

The teacher stood over him with a look of fury on
his face. "Don't bother to try to excuse yourself," he

snapped. "I know it was something to do with a dog — it always is with you. Since you're so fascinated by dogs, Neil, you can spend the weekend writing an essay for me about dogs in Roman times. Your test didn't reveal an extensive knowledge of the Romans as people, so I suppose Roman dogs are better than nothing at all!"

"The history of dogs in ancient Rome, eh? It's just what you always wanted to study, wasn't it?" Chris Wilson laughed when Neil told him about the essay that Mr. Hamley told him to write. They were both heading toward home after school had finished.

"I don't know where to start," grumbled Neil.

"Don't look so down about it. You've got enough worries at the moment. I'll give you a hand. We'll go back to your place and see what's on the Internet. There's bound to be loads of stuff on there about it."

When they got back to King Street Kennels, Chris sat down at the computer and accessed one of the biggest Internet search engines. Neil sat beside him at the desk and stocked up the printer with paper.

DOGS + ROMANS, typed Chris. The screen instantly told him that the search engine had found over three thousand references to dogs and Romans.

"Maybe we'd be better with CD-ROMs," Neil suggested. "There's a couple in the library that are bound to have something. I could go tomorrow."

Chris held up his hand. "Hang on. Give me half an hour with this thing and I'll narrow down the search. It's all on here if you know where to look for it."

Neil wondered what he'd do without the technical genius of his friend. "Cool. I'll go and get us some drinks. Workers need energy!"

As Neil walked into the kitchen he noticed the change in his mother's manner. She was smiling and looked more relaxed than she had for days. "Good news!" she confirmed, beaming at him. "The doctors have identified what's wrong with Sarah. She's got salmonella — a very bad case of food poisoning. She's on some really strong antibiotics and she's beginning to get better already. If she keeps it up, she should be home early next week."

Neil felt dizzy with relief. "That's terrific!"

Emily looked up from her studies at the table. "It's great news, isn't it?"

"What did she eat to get that?" asked Neil. "Dad's pasta is usually fairly poison-free."

"The doctors think it was something she ate on her school field trip last week. A couple of the other children also had upset stomachs but Sarah had it the worst. Her symptoms were so confusing at first."

"Well, I'm glad she's getting better," said Neil, smiling.

"There's only one thing," Carole went on. "She

asked for that photo of Lucky that we took for the website, but I couldn't find it in the office. Do either of you know where it is?"

Emily and Neil looked at each other. Neil fumbled for the picture in his pocket and handed it to his mother.

"What were you doing with it?" she asked, gazing at him intently. Then she narrowed her eyes. "The two of you were going to look for Lucky, weren't you?" As Neil slowly nodded, she shook her head. "Leave it to the police and the SPCA," she said firmly. "Even though Sarah doesn't have rabies, the dog could still be dangerous. I don't want either of you to take any risks." Then she stopped and fully appreciated for the first time how grubby Neil was looking. "And you'd better go and wash, Neil. What on earth were you doing at school today?"

Neil left the kitchen clutching two cold cans of soda. Emily followed him outside.

Sam came bounding up to them from his favorite spot underneath the garden hedge. Emily shied away as Neil bent over to pat him. "I can't risk giving him my infection," she said, waving her gloved hand at Neil.

"Trust you to get ringworm," he said.

Emily's face shaded. "It's just bad luck. You could have gotten it just as easily as me."

"I'm glad I didn't," Neil said. "C'mon, I want to

check on Jimbo." As they walked into the rescue center, a cacophony of barks greeted them. The Airedale terrier still looked fairly lifeless.

Emily gazed at the sad dog. "What are we going to do about Lucky? Mom's told us not to look for her."

Neil thought for a moment. "She didn't. Not really. At least, not exactly. She just told us not to take any risks, that's all."

The food in Jimbo's bowl had hardly been touched, although the big, shaggy dog was curled proprietorially over Sarah's old sweater. Neil's heart lurched when he saw the pain in the dog's eyes. He opened the gate of the pen and tickled Jimbo's graying chin. Emily stood well back. "Sarah's getting better," he told the dog. "She should be back very soon. We'll soon find you a new home when we've got an adorable picture of you, won't we?"

"I've been thinking," Emily said. "About Lucky. Maybe we could put an appeal about her on the website. We can show her picture and ask if anybody out there has seen her."

Neil grinned. "There aren't a lot of people around here who are on the Internet, but it's worth a try. Chris is here now — he'll help us do it."

Back in the office, Neil slapped Chris on the back and offered him a drink. "Change of plan. We need your help with an urgent Internet appeal."

Chris laughed. "Good thing I'd finished getting all the info I needed for your essay, then, isn't it?"

Neil explained Emily's idea and together they helped copy Lucky's picture from the home page of the King Street Kennels website and paste it onto the rescue center page.

Emily typed in the appeal as it would appear on screen to anybody who accessed the page.

HAVE YOU SEEN THIS DOG?
PLEASE TELL US WHERE AND WHEN.
E-MAIL PUPPYPATROL@KSK.CO.UK
OR PHONE COMPTON-26547.

"That should do it," she said. "I'll print out some copies of this page and we'll use it tomorrow when we ask around. Julie's helping us, and so are some of the others from my class."

"What if it *was* Lucky that I heard in Padsham?" Neil asked.

"Well, then, we'll go to Padsham after we've covered Compton and Colshaw," Emily said. "We have to try everywhere."

Emily broke off to answer the phone that was ringing. "King Street Kennels. Can I help you?"

Neil listened to Emily's side of the conversation and his pulse quickened. It was one of her classmates. It sounded like she had some news about the whereabouts of Lucky. Emily replaced the receiver and jumped up.

"Breakthrough! We've had a positive sighting. My friend thinks she saw Kay Davis and Lucky walking along the road where she lives in Compton. They went into a house just around the corner from her."

"Was she sure it was Lucky?"

"The dog had a curly coat and curly ears, and her owner looks exactly like Kay. We'll go there first thing tomorrow when it's light and then you'll see. I'm sure it's Lucky, I really am! Neil, I think we've found her."

CHAPTER SEVEN

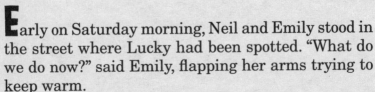

Early on Saturday morning, Neil and Emily stood in the street where Lucky had been spotted. "What do we do now?" said Emily, flapping her arms trying to keep warm.

Neil scratched his head. He wasn't sure himself. He was just about to suggest knocking on doors when a police car turned onto the road. Neil and Emily reacted simultaneously and ducked behind a dense hedge just as Sergeant Moorhead pulled up outside a house nearby and got out.

Neil looked at Emily and held a finger to his lips. "How come he's here, too?" whispered Emily.

Neil shrugged. "Maybe they also had a tip-off?"

The policeman knocked firmly at the door of the house. A dog barked, then a woman answered it.

"That didn't sound much like Lucky," Emily whispered.

Neil told her to hush again as he tried to listen to what was being said. The woman shook her head vigorously in response to the policeman's inquiries and then she went back indoors. A moment later she returned with a tiny little dog. Sure enough, its hair was curly and its ears were, too — but it was a poodle.

Neil and Emily groaned.

"It does look a bit like Lucky," Emily pointed out.

"Only if you need glasses," Neil replied.

The police drove off after a couple of minutes and Neil and Emily emerged from hiding, picking leaves

off their jackets and their jeans. "What now?" Emily asked.

"I'm going to go talk to that woman in Wolsten-home Row who knows Kay, then I'll go home and check the e-mails."

"In that case, I'll start asking around and showing people that leaflet," Emily said.

"Make sure you point out that Lucky isn't a poo-dle! I'll see you later this afternoon. Don't forget, we're going to see Squirt."

"I won't forget. But we've got to find Lucky, Neil. If Sergeant Moorhead got here before us, he might be closer to her than we think. Lucky stands a better chance if we get to her first!"

Chris Wilson arrived on his bike at King Street Kennels just after lunch. He took some papers out of his backpack, then ran into the office. Neil was sitting at the computer, having just established an Internet connection.

"Here you are," exclaimed Chris triumphantly, waving the papers in front of Neil's face. "Five hundred words on dogs in Roman times. I've knocked that raw info I got off the Internet into shape for you."

Neil quickly flicked through it. "I hope it's not too good! You know Mr. Hamley. He'd never believe it if I got something completely correct."

"I don't see why not," Chris said. "The teachers are

always raving on about the wonders of new technology. This just proves that you know how to use it."

"It proves *you* know how to use it," Neil said. "But thanks, buddy, that's great."

"So how's the hunt going?" Chris asked. "Are you any closer to finding Lucky?"

Neil shrugged helplessly. "Not really. We had a false alarm early this morning, and a close call with Sergeant Moorhead. He's one step ahead of us at the moment. Emily is in town now, showing people Lucky's picture."

"That might turn up something."

"Possibly. I did go over to see that woman I met the other day. The one in Wolstenhome Row behind the school."

"And what did she have to say?" asked Chris, raising an eyebrow.

"Oh, it was hardly inspiring stuff. She couldn't remember much else. Kay rented the house and had kept pretty much to herself."

"Hmm. What about the Internet message we posted last night?"

"I was just about to check." Neil accessed the kennel's website and opened up the e-mail application. His spirits soared when he found twenty-two messages flash up. He slumped back in his chair when he discovered that they all came from places like Omaha, Nebraska, and Jacksonville in Florida. There was even one from Honolulu in Hawaii. He ruffled his hair in despair. "Unless Kay has skipped the country again these will all be useless."

"If she *has* skipped the country, it's no longer our problem, is it?" Chris joked. "Seriously, Neil, all you're going to get overnight on the Internet is stuff from America. The time difference means that when we're asleep, they're all surfing the World Wide Web. If you wait a little longer you'll probably get some replies from the UK."

"Maybe," Neil mumbled, "but I can't help thinking there's more we could do."

"Do you have any more leads at all?"

"Just the taxicab connection. Kay Davis left here last week in a cab. I can't remember the name of the company, but it definitely had a red sign on top."

"Problem solved. That's Anniston's on Goldhawk Lane near the train station. My dad uses them sometimes."

"Great! What do we do now? Should I just call up and ask where they took her?"

"I don't think they'd tell you that over the phone. You could be anyone! Ask them face-to-face."

"Great. But I can't go this afternoon." Neil looked at the clock on the office wall. "We're all going to see Sarah in an hour. It'll have to wait."

Sarah managed a smile as Neil and Emily walked into the children's ward at Compton Hospital. She looked very pale against the white sheets of her bed.

"Hi, Squirt," Neil said, struggling to return her smile. They only had ten minutes with her because she was still very tired.

"I've got a surprise for you," Emily said, handing Sarah a card. When Sarah opened it, Neil noticed that Emily had signed it FUDGE along with a tiny paw print.

Sarah's eyes gleamed. "Is Fudge missing me?" she asked.

"Of course," Emily said. "We told him you're coming home soon, and he's looking forward to that. He plays on his exercise wheel, but he won't do any of his tricks for me."

The photograph of Lucky was propped up on Sarah's bedside locker. Sarah saw Neil looking at it. "What's the matter with Lucky?" she asked. "Mom looked really upset when I asked how she was."

"Nothing," Neil and Emily said in unison.

Sarah looked at them disbelievingly. Her chin wobbled in a sure sign that tears were on their way. Neil gripped her little hand firmly. "I promise you, Sarah," he said. "Nothing bad is going to happen to Lucky."

Sarah looked deep into his eyes. "Cross your heart?"

"Cross my heart," Neil repeated, feeling very guilty as he watched Sarah's face light up with relief. Neil had to double his efforts at trying to find Lucky now — before Sarah returned home and got a dreadful surprise.

Sergeant Moorhead was at King Street Kennels when Emily and Neil returned from their hospital visit in the car.

Bob Parker stepped out of the Range Rover and greeted the policeman warmly. "Any luck finding the dog?" Bob asked him, shaking his hand.

"Not yet, Bob," the policeman replied. "I've asked around Compton without success, so I think she's somewhere in Colshaw or Padsham."

Neil glanced at Emily. "I told you they're in Padsham," he hissed.

"Have you had any firm sightings, Sergeant Moorhead?" asked Emily slyly.

"Well, yes, we have, actually."

Neil and Emily tensed. Would it be a new lead or something they already knew about?

"A woman was spotted up on the ridgeway this afternoon. She had trouble getting her dog back into a small blue car. The descriptions seemed perfect. We're running checks on it now. I don't think it'll take long to find her if it was them."

Neil and Emily looked at each other and gulped. They raced across to the kennel's office and closed the door firmly behind them. "We're losing the battle, Em. We need some luck to come our way — and quick."

Emily sat in her mother's swivel chair and put her feet up on the desk. She leaned back with her hands behind her head. "Julie gave us something that might help. She called her cousin in Paris and found out some e-mail addresses. One of them is the French equivalent of the SPCA and another is a dog shelter. There are others, too. Lucky might have been a rescue dog and somebody might remember him. We can e-mail them right away, if you like."

Neil scratched his head and then booted up the computer. "It's worth a try."

As he copied out messages to send to France, Neil filled Emily in on the conversation he had with the old woman in Compton and about the taxi connection.

"Are you up for a little trip into town tonight — under the cover of darkness?" Neil pretended to shiver.

"It's a bit shady, isn't it? Mom would never let us go if she knew what we were up to."

Neil chuckled as he continued to tap away on the computer keyboard. He hit the SEND button with a flourish and dispatched the bunch of help messages instantaneously. He turned and faced Emily with his most cunning grin. "She won't know. I can tell her we've gone down the road to see Chris. We'll set off and ride our bikes in the direction of his house." He paused for effect before continuing. "Then we'll just keep on going into Compton."

Emily rolled her eyes. "I hope you know what you're doing, Neil Parker — because I have absolutely no idea!"

CHAPTER EIGHT

Later that evening, Neil and Emily walked into An-niston's taxi office near Compton railway station. There was a woman sitting at a radio microphone, with a man standing just behind her.

"Hi," said Neil. "I was hoping you could help me. You picked up a woman last Tuesday night, and brought her to King Street Kennels to pick up a dog. The driver would remember the dog, because it was panicking and barking a lot. Can you tell us where you took them?"

The man stepped forward, folding his well-muscled, heavily tattooed arms. "Why d'you want to know?"

"I live at King Street Kennels," Neil explained. "She left something there and I want to give it to her."

"The police have already been in asking the same question," he said darkly. "And I told them what I'm telling you now. The ride wasn't a booking. She came into the office here, so we don't have a record of where it went. Now off you go, the pair of you, and stop wasting my time."

Neil and Emily retreated back into the street. "That wasn't much help," grumbled Emily.

Neil wasn't about to give in and was thinking hard. He was sure that he'd recognize the cab that had picked up Kay and Lucky if he saw it again. He scanned the line of cars waiting outside the cab office but didn't spot it. Neil voiced his thought to his sister.

"It'll probably turn up later," Emily said. "Should we wait here for a while? I bet we can stay out a bit longer without being missed."

Half an hour later they were still waiting. Neil looked at his watch. It was eight o'clock. Then a quarter past. He prayed that the taxi company would get busy soon. The line of cabs outside the office hadn't moved for ages.

Two cabs had left and although two new ones had joined the line, the cab that had brought Kay Davis still had not appeared. "We'll have to go home soon," he said.

Emily was staring at the brightly lit window of the

office. "New cabs only seem to arrive when others drive off. I think they must like to keep a certain number outside the office at any one time. They do seem to get a lot of people coming over from the station."

"I guess so," Neil said, as Emily's gaze shifted to the phone booth at the end of the road. "Do you think we should call one? Or three?"

"I don't want us to get into any trouble, Neil."

"Neither do I. But do we have a choice?"

Neil handed Emily a coin and she ran down to the phone. Sure enough, when the man in the office had taken the call, the cab at the front of the line moved off.

"Fingers crossed," Emily said as she joined him again. Another cab drove up a couple of minutes later, but it wasn't the cab that had picked up Lucky. Neil groaned. He only had one more coin left.

"It's worth another try," Emily said.

Neil went to the phone and asked the man in the office to send a cab to the bus station to collect a Miss Dotty Hamley. "I sent it off to look for Mr. Hamley's dog," he said when he got back. "I feel really guilty about it."

Emily bit her lip. "I sent mine to that awful woman who lives next door to Julie."

They waited hopefully for a couple of minutes, then the car that had brought Kay Davis suddenly appeared at the end of the row. "Yes!" Neil cried. "That's the one! It was that color and I think I recognize the driver, too."

Neil and Emily ran over to talk to the driver.

"Excuse me. Can you help us, please? We need to find that lady you brought to King Street Kennels on Tuesday night," Neil said.

The driver frowned.

"Please," Emily pleaded. "We live at the kennels, and we're trying to find her because there's a chance her dog got ringworm there." She waved her hand in its protective glove in the man's face. "It can be nasty if it's not treated properly. We just want to tell her to take the dog to the vet."

"That was the woman the police were asking about," the driver said suspiciously, shrinking back into the car away from Emily's hand. "They came by this afternoon interviewing some of the drivers."

"This is nothing to do with the police," Neil replied quickly. "I promise you, I only want to talk to her."

The driver studied him as if he was trying to work out whether Neil was telling the truth or not. Neil met his gaze steadily. The driver shrugged. "I don't honestly know where she lives. I picked her up here and her dog was making such a fuss in the back that she asked me to drop her off on Padsham High Street. She said she'd walk from there."

"So you've no idea where she went?" Emily asked desperately.

"None at all."

They thanked him and then rushed back across the street before any angry cab drivers returned.

"This is great," Neil gasped, as they hurriedly unlocked their bikes. "We've got a lead on the police. We know Kay lives in Padsham, and they don't!"

"So the cabdriver didn't tell you *exactly* where he dropped her off?" Chris asked on Sunday morning. "High Street is half a mile long!"

Neil grinned sheepishly.

The Padsham Sunday craft market was in full swing. Two multicolored lines of stalls laden with assorted jams and pickles, wines and wickerwork, ran up both sides of the street. Only a narrow aisle was left between them and it was already throbbing with busy shoppers. "You start on one side, and I'll start on the other," Neil said, when they'd left their bikes chained to a lamppost. "We'll meet up again at the end." He handed Chris some of the posters that Emily had printed off from the website with the picture of Lucky and then he set off.

Neil pushed his way through a throng of people at a stall where a man was offering a tasting of country wine. On the other side, he saw a woman standing alone and decided to try her first.

"Sorry," she said, when Neil showed her Lucky's picture, "I'm not from here. I've come down for the day from Manchester." The next two people he spoke

to said the same thing. When he finally found a man from Padsham, the man shook his head and said he was allergic to dogs.

"It's just too busy," Chris said, when they met up again. "Ninety percent of the people aren't even from Padsham — they've just come for the market. I didn't realize it was this popular."

Neil thought quickly. "You try the park, then, and I'll go to the river walk where I heard Lucky." After separating for the second time, Neil walked right along the riverbank and then back again, but there was still no sign of the dog or Kay.

"Still no luck," Chris said, shortly before lunchtime. "I even tried directory assistance a few minutes ago to see if there was a new listing for Kay Davis but there wasn't."

Neil sighed.

"That's not the worst of it," Chris said. "There was a policeman in the park. It seemed like he was asking questions to dog owners."

"Oh, no!" Neil groaned. "They're bound to find Lucky before we do. We need another break. And fast!"

Emily was waiting for Neil when he got back to King Street Kennels. "Come quickly!" she said. "Some e-mails have come in."

Neil followed her into the office. The e-mail icon on the computer screen was blinking. He clicked on the icon, then the first e-mail appeared on the screen. He looked at it closely, then he groaned.

Emily squinted at the screen. "Oh, no!" she wailed. "They're in French. What do we do now, Neil?"

Neil gritted his teeth and hit the print button. In all, there were eight e-mails from Paris. Only two were in English. One was from a dog shelter and the other was from an animal welfare society. Neither of them knew anything about Lucky. Of the six in French, five were short, but one was longer and looked distinctly promising.

Emily reviewed the shorter e-mails. "These don't

look too complicated," she said. "Julie knows a little French. I could call her and read it out to her. Maybe she'd understand it."

"OK," Neil said. He got up to find a French dictionary and a phrase book. When he got back, he began to laboriously translate the long e-mail, looking up one word at a time. Emily was spelling out another, word by word, over the phone to Julie.

After ten minutes, he realized that the first line of his e-mail merely thanked him for the e-mail he'd sent. He sighed and began to struggle with the second line.

Emily put the phone down. "These ones just say thank you and not much else," she said. "They don't know anything but they'll let us know if they see a dog like that around."

Neil frowned as he looked up the meaning of the word *connais*. He found out it was from the verb "to know." His eyes scanned the rest of the e-mail and the name Kay jumped out at him, followed by Annie and Lucky.

"Yes!" he cried. "There's something in this one, Em."

Emily took the e-mail and phoned Julie again. Neil waited impatiently as she spelled the words out. Moments later, a broad smile spread over Emily's face. "Thanks a million, Julie," she said, putting the phone down.

"Come on," Neil urged. "What did it say?"

"OK. It's from a rescue center in Paris. Earlier this year they successfully homed an abandoned puppy exactly like the one in the picture with somebody called Kay Laurent. . . ."

"Laurent must be Kay's married name. It's got to be!" Neil grabbed the phone and called directory assistance, but there was no listing for a Mrs. Laurent anywhere in the local area.

"We're out of luck again," he said despondently.

"We're not out of luck at all," Emily replied. "We're in luck. If you'd just let me finish, the message also says that the dog was actually called Lou-Lou and the new owner had bought it for her five-year-old daughter. We know Kay lives in Padsham, so we might be able to find her easily tomorrow."

Neil folded his arms. "Just how are we going to do that?"

"Easy. We go to the nursery school in Padsham and she's bound to be there."

"We've got to be at school tomorrow, too. So how are we supposed to get to Padsham? There'll be dozens of little girls there. How do we know which one is her?"

Emily thought for a moment, then she picked up the phone book to look up a number. "A boy in my class moved to Padsham last year," she said. "I'll call him and ask him to ask around." She smiled brightly. "Come on, Neil. It's the best lead we've had so far!"

Reluctantly, Neil started to smile.

* * *

Neil put his hands in his pockets and walked out
into the sunshine. Sam ran up to him, his tail wagging wildly in anticipation of a walk, so Neil took
him along the ridgeway. On the way back, he saw the
white SPCA van driving toward the kennel, so he
ran home with Sam leaping along at his heels.

Terry McCall was just coming out of the office
when he got there. As Sam wagged his tail in wel-
come, she reached down to ruffle his coat. "That's a
fine dog you've got there, Neil," she said.

"Thanks," Neil said proudly. "Sam came into the
rescue center as a pup and we decided to keep him."
His face changed as he thought of Jimbo. "I wish we
could give all the other dogs a home, too," he said
sadly.

"I know." The SPCA inspector smiled. "It's the
hardest part of the job, but you have to say no sometimes. Your father told me you're having problems
with an Airedale terrier. I was passing by, so I
thought I'd come to have a look."

Neil took her over to the rescue center. "His owner
died recently, and he's very listless," he said. "The
only person he responds to is my little sister Sarah.
I was hoping to get a really lively picture of him to
put on our website, but then Sarah got sick. Jimbo's
missing her an awful lot. More than we expected.
He's taking a long time to get over it."

"Hmm," Terry McCall said, as they reached

Jimbo's pen. She opened the gate, then she held her hand out to the dog. "Hello, Jimbo," she said cheerfully. As usual, the Airedale just opened one eye. Very gently, the SPCA inspector felt his coat, then she tickled his chin. Jimbo gazed at her for a moment, then he wagged his tail, just once.

"He's thin but he's healthy enough," she said, as they walked away from Jimbo's pen.

"We're hoping that Sarah'll be home from the hospital tomorrow," Neil said. "When we get him on the website, I'll ask for a home that's got a daughter of about Sarah's age."

"Dogs are very loyal to their owners," Terry McCall said thoughtfully. "Jimbo might think that he's being disloyal by being friendly with someone else, especially someone who reminds him of his owner. He should get over it in time. You're doing a good job with him, anyway, Neil."

Neil smiled as they walked out into the late afternoon sunshine. Just then, Emily raced out of the office. Neil held his finger to his lips to warn her to keep quiet. "Do you know how the search for Kay Davis is going?" he asked Terry.

"I talked to Sergeant Moorhead on my way here," she said. "They've drawn a blank in Compton and in Colshaw but they're pretty sure the dog is in Padsham now. They're going to start looking there tomorrow. Sergeant Moorhead thinks he'll find them very soon." Emily and Neil glanced at each other.

"Well, I'd better be off now," said Terry. "Thanks for showing me around, Neil. We're always looking for volunteers to help out at our place in Colshaw. Maybe the two of you would like to come over sometime?"

"Yes, please!" they cried in unison.

As soon as the SPCA van drove off, Emily clutched Neil's arm. "I've got some news," she said. "There's a girl named Annie Laurent who started at Padsham Preschool a couple of weeks ago. She speaks some

English, but she also speaks perfect French. Before she came here, she used to live in Paris! And the best of it is, Annie's got a puppy called Lou-Lou!"

Neil grinned. "Well done, Em! We've cracked it. We've found Lucky at last."

"As long as the police don't get there first," Emily said cautiously.

CHAPTER NINE

"**D**o you know how much a quarantine costs, Mom?" Neil asked Carole over their late dinner on Sunday night.

"A small fortune," Carole replied.

"Is it cheaper if the dog comes from France?" Emily asked casually, popping a French fry into her mouth.

"It's just the same," Carole said. "At the moment, any dog that comes into the UK from abroad has to go into quarantine for six months. The regulations are very strict. Each dog's got to be kept in total isolation. It's terrible for them. Your dad's got a friend who runs a quarantine kennel. He does his best, but he says it's a heartbreaking job."

"So we couldn't quarantine a dog here?" Neil added.

Carole shook her head vigorously. "We don't have a license, or the right facilities. Why?"

"Oh, no reason," muttered Emily. "We can't help thinking about Lucky, that's all. It'll be awful if she has to be put down."

"I know," Carole said as she divided an apple pie into portions. "I feel terrible about it, too. However, we can't afford to take any risks when there's even the remotest possibility that a dog has rabies. It wasn't just Sarah, that woman put us all in danger — and the other dogs in the kennels, too. It really was a very selfish thing for her to do." Carole shrugged helplessly. "There's nothing we can do now."

Bob arrived back from the hospital just as everybody had finished their supper. "Sorry I'm late. Sarah has made friends with another girl in her ward," he said, smiling. "She asked me why I kept on hanging around!"

Neil laughed. "Typical Sarah."

"I decided to come home for a real dinner," Bob said, rubbing his belly. "I've had enough hospital food. Anything left? And what's this about there being nothing we can do now?"

Emily looked at Bob. "It's Lucky," she said. "If Kay Davis can't pay the quarantine fees when the police find her, the dog will be put down, won't she?"

"For all we know," said Neil, "the dog could have already been vaccinated against rabies — so she might not be any risk to us, anyway."

"We were wondering if we could do anything to help," said Emily. "We feel so useless."

Bob Parker frowned as he thought about it. "I'm not thrilled about it, either, but I don't know what we can do. I know someone near Manchester who's got a quarantine facility. He might take Lucky in. But this is still all academic. We don't know where she lives, so we can't get in touch with her. I think it's best if we let the police locate her and let them decide how to handle everything."

Neil and Emily glanced at each other. Neither of them said a word.

Just before Neil and Emily went to bed that night, they sat up in Emily's bedroom and speculated about the next day. One way or another it was probably going to decide Lucky's fate. Neil and Emily were convinced that their latest clue about the French girl in Padsham Preschool would lead them straight to Lou-Lou. However, the police were closing in on Lou-Lou just as fast.

"I just remembered something," said Emily, hesitantly.

"What's that?"

"There was a cat outside school the other week. It looked lost, so I picked it up to see if there was a tag on its collar. It wriggled away before I could check. I'd completely forgotten about it. That's probably where I got my ringworm." She waved her gloved hands in Neil's face.

Neil turned his head. "Get away!"

"Despite what Dad said, Lucky deserves one last chance," said Emily. "And so does Kay. If she's got a daughter, I bet she'd want to make sure that Lucky was vaccinated against rabies."

"Lou-Lou, you mean," said Neil despondently. "I don't know, Em. I'm not sure how it's going to turn out tomorrow. Padsham's half an hour away by bike. There's no way I can get there before school starts, and nursery schools close early — so I can't get there in the afternoon, either. We have track tomorrow afternoon, and you know what Mr. Hamley is like."

"We have to try," Emily said doggedly. "Sarah's coming home tomorrow. If anything happened to Lucky it wouldn't help her recovery at all."

"We could tell Dad about Annie and the school," Emily said. "But he might tell Sergeant Moorhead."

"He'd probably think he had to." Neil thought for a moment. "There's only one thing I can do. I'll take a slight detour on our cross-country run tomorrow. If I take my bike I'll get to Padsham in time to meet Annie Laurent at school. She shouldn't be too difficult to spot and Kay will probably be there to get her. If not, someone else will be; I'll just follow them home."

"Mr. Hamley will be furious if he finds out," Emily

said. "You're in enough trouble as it is. And Mom and Dad would ground you for a year!"

"That's a risk I'll have to take," said Neil grimly. "And at least I'll get out of cross-country!"

"I hope no one has forgotten their gear today," said Mr. Hamley on Monday afternoon. "The course I'm going to suggest for our afternoon cross-country run is going to be very challenging and shouldn't be missed!"

Neil was the only pupil in the schoolroom not grumbling. He'd been waiting anxiously for this moment all day. In the changing room, he put on his shorts, then he wrapped his pants underneath his baggy sweater. Hasheem beamed at him. He knew what Neil was planning. "Are you ready?" he asked.

"As ready as I'll ever be," Neil replied, as they went outside and set off at a steady pace. Mr. Hamley was standing at the school gates with a stopwatch in his hand. The teacher seemed to stare at him as he approached the gates and then ran past. "You're putting on weight, Neil Parker. Let's see you run some of it off this afternoon."

Hasheem chuckled. "Little does he know that you're going to set a world record for the slowest time!"

Neil kept his head down until they had turned the first corner on the route they were meant to follow.

Hasheem shouted, "Good luck!" to Neil as they separated and he doubled back to get his bike.

Neil pedaled away from the school as quickly as he could. Only when he was on the far side of Compton did he pause for breath and stop to put his pants back on. It was ten past two and he had plenty of time to get to Padsham Preschool. The route took him through green fields and countryside and he began to whistle as he rode along.

At the bottom of Padsham High Street, he suddenly skidded to a halt. Sergeant Moorhead was talking to one of his officers on the pavement outside a pet shop. Neil dismounted, hung his head, and

prayed he hadn't been seen. His heart began to beat faster when the policeman called out and waved him over. "Hello, Neil," he said. "You're a long way from home!"

"Ye-es," Neil croaked. "What are you doing here?"

Sergeant Moorhead glowered at him for a moment, then he winked. "I think I've found our fugitive dog," he said. "I've got just a couple more addresses to check out with my colleague here."

"Er, good luck," Neil mumbled, cycling away as quickly as his shaky legs would take him. His heart was racing.

Padsham Preschool was in an annex next to the main primary school. Neil was relieved that the policemen were nowhere to be seen when he arrived, but he didn't have any time to waste. He didn't want Kay Davis — or Kay Laurent — to see him before he saw her, so he found a place at the side of the school near a wall where he could observe the whole street.

Some parents had already begun to arrive to pick up their children. As time passed, Neil began to panic. His eyes constantly scanned the road for the police as he waited for Kay to arrive. When children started to come out of the school, he began to despair.

Suddenly, he saw Kay. She was walking along the road toward him with a dog on a leash. Neil recognized Lou-Lou immediately. The Pumi was very distinctive. A little girl with dark brown hair in a ponytail ran up to her outside the main gate. As she hugged Kay, Lou-Lou jumped up and licked her on the cheek.

A flash of white caught his eye at the top of the road. Sergeant Moorhead's police car had just turned onto the road and was slowly making its way toward the school.

Neil raced across the road with his bike and pounced on Kay and the girl. "Hurry up!" he said, grabbing Kay's arm. "We've got to hurry! For Lou-Lou's sake!"

CHAPTER TEN

For a moment, the woman and her daughter looked astonished. Lou-Lou started to bark. Then a flash of recognition flitted across her face. "You're the boy from King Street Kennels," Kay said. "What on earth's the matter?"

Neil took a deep breath. As he began to speak, the puppy recognized him and jumped up playfully, a little brown bundle of curls. Neil told Kay all about the drama of the last few days and about the health scare at King Street Kennels. All the time he spoke, he was tugging them along — away from the approaching police car.

"Oh, no! Lou-Lou's been inoculated. There was never any risk of anyone getting rabies!" Kay cried.

"But nobody knew that," said Neil.

The little girl looked at Neil quizzically, and then she said something in French. Kay replied and then she turned back to Neil, shaking her head sorrowfully. "I can explain everything if you give me a chance. We live just around the corner. I can drive you home later."

"There isn't time," said Neil urgently. "The police are just about to turn up." He thought for a moment. "Why don't you come to the kennel instead? We can work out what you need to do. My dad can help you with sorting out Lou-Lou's quarantine. If you can get my bike into your car you can tell me about it on the way."

"OK," Kay said. She clutched her daughter's hand and they hurried down the road. Neil pulled Lou-Lou along — she was no bother and even seemed to be enjoying all the excitement.

Two streets away Kay stopped in front of a blue car. "It'll be a tight squeeze, I'm afraid," she said as she opened the trunk. The bike just fit in, but the door of the trunk wouldn't close so she had to tie it down to the bumper with a piece of rope.

Lou-Lou shied away from the car. Seeing the dog's distress, Annie began to get upset. The dog was still having problems with enclosed spaces. Kay talked to her daughter as Neil tried to calm the frightened dog. He felt terribly sorry for both of them. When Annie's tears had stopped, she went and sat in the car. "I'll just go and get Lou-Lou's vaccination certificate," Kay said, and rushed into her house.

When Kay came back, she lifted the dog firmly into the backseat. The trembling animal huddled against Annie for comfort as Neil got into the front seat.

"She had a terrible time on the journey over," Kay said, starting the engine. "It took over six hours and she was stuck in a box underneath the seat. I got a tranquilizer for her from the vet in Paris but it didn't work very well."

"We wondered if that was why she's frightened of cars," Neil said. The car pulled away from the curb and headed out of Padsham. "Did you take her for a walk by the river the other day? And on the ridge-way in Compton?"

Kay nodded. "I was trying to get her used to the car, but it didn't help much." She handed him the vaccination certificate. It was similar to others that Neil had seen, except it had the words *La Rage* written underneath the other diseases that Lou-Lou had been vaccinated against. A sticker gave the batch number of the vaccine the French vet had used. There was also a Petrac label with an identification number on it.

"Lou-Lou's been microchipped," Kay said. "We had an identification chip implanted into the skin behind her head. That proves the certificate belongs to her."

"Where did the other one come from, then? The one you gave Dad?"

Kay's face shaded. "Lucky was my mother's dog."

"Oh. *Katherine* Davis was your mom."

"They both died in a car crash a few months ago. Lucky was just a puppy, too."

"I'm sorry," Neil said.

Kay turned into Padsham High Street just as Sergeant Moorhead's police car turned into the street they'd left. Neil ducked down quickly and the policeman didn't seem to notice him.

"I married a man I met in Paris," Kay explained.

"But my marriage broke up just before my mother died." Her expression was a mixture of anger and sadness. Neil didn't know what to say. Kay Davis had had an awful time, but it didn't excuse the risk she had taken.

"It must have been tough," he mumbled sympathetically.

Kay nodded. "These things happen. I had to come home for Dad. He insisted on selling the house he'd owned with Mom, but he's got arthritis and he needed an operation. I didn't think he could cope alone. Annie was heartbroken when I told her Lou-Lou would have to go into quarantine for six months. When I found out what it was going to cost, I realized I couldn't afford it. My husband left us virtually penniless and I knew Dad had nothing. That's when I decided to smuggle Lou-Lou into England. I know it wasn't the right thing to do, but I didn't have much choice. It wasn't as if Lou-Lou was a risk or anything."

"Maybe," Neil said, "but my little sister Sarah was taken into the hospital with a mystery illness the day after you collected Lou-Lou. Then Emily got ringworm, and Dad was worried that Lou-Lou might have it, too. That's how we first found out the vaccination certificate was false. Emily and I were worried about Lou-Lou. There's been a case of parvo in Compton, so we decided to try to find you. When we suspected that you had smuggled Lou-Lou in from France we had to tell the police."

"I understand," Kay said. She sighed as she drove. "It's such an awful mess, isn't it? I'm so sorry Lou-Lou has caused everybody so much trouble."

"Why did you bring Lou-Lou to us, anyway?"

"I had to go back to Paris to finalize some matters to do with my separation," said Kay. "It was all a mad rush and I took Annie with me, but Dad had just had his operation so I couldn't leave Lou-Lou with him."

Neil nodded. It all made sense now, but he was afraid it was too late.

Kay's lips pursed. "Don't worry," she said, "it was bound to come out anyway. Someone would have realized sooner or later. Annie's going to be so upset while Lou-Lou's away, but I've got a part-time job now. It'll be a struggle, but at least I can manage to pay the bills."

Neil smiled, but he was thinking that Kay and Lou-Lou's problems might not be that easy to solve.

Bob Parker's face was expressionless when Neil appeared with Kay, Lou-Lou, and little Annie at King Street Kennels. "Dad," Neil said quickly, "Lou-Lou has been inoculated against rabies. Kay's got a certificate to prove it. I found them in Padsham."

"I'm terribly sorry to have caused you such trouble," Kay mumbled, as she scooped up her dog who had just jumped out of the car. "If you give me a chance, I'll try to explain why."

"You'd better come into the office," Bob said, then he turned to Neil. "You've been busy this afternoon, Neil. How have you managed to ride to Padsham already?" Bob looked at his watch. "Did school finish early today?"

Neil's face fell. "Not exactly."

Bob Parker didn't look happy. "I'll talk to you about this later, Neil. In the meantime, why don't you take this young lady and show her around?" He had closed the office door firmly behind them before Neil had a chance to object. Annie looked up at Neil and grinned. Neil thought she'd probably get on very well with Squirt.

Emily came running out of the house, still dressed in her school clothes. "What's going on?" she asked. "I just got back when I saw you arrive."

"I found them," Neil said. "They were at the school. Lou-Lou has been inoculated against rabies. Kay's had a terrible time. She's talking to Dad now. I just hope that he'll be able to help."

Emily took Annie to see the puppies in the rescue center as a worried Neil got his bike out of the trunk of the car. As Neil crossed the courtyard, Emily appeared at the door of the rescue center and shouted over to him. "Neil, come and see this!" she cried.

Neil trudged over, his hands in his pockets. "Hurry up!" Emily said, grabbing his arm to usher him inside.

Jimbo was in the aisle of the rescue center, his tail wagging happily as he pawed at a rubber ball that Annie was holding. Little Annie was laughing, her sadness over Lou-Lou's distress forgotten.

"I'm going to get the camera," Emily said, as Neil watched the little girl and the dog. When she came back, she took a couple of excellent Polaroids of Jimbo, then they took Annie and Jimbo outside for some proper exercise in the field. The old dog retrieved a ball that Annie threw for him, and chased after it again when Annie kicked it away for a second time.

As Neil and Emily watched, Bob came out of the office to join them. He scratched his chin. "It's quite a story, I must admit. You both must've had quite a struggle to find them. I wish you had told me more about what you were up to."

"Sorry, Dad. We decided that Lou-Lou deserved a chance," said Emily. "Are you going to help them?"

Bob nodded. "I'll try. I've called my friend and he's agreed to take the dog for her quarantine period. It's not too far away so Kay will be able to visit regularly with Annie. Mike's coming over to check the microchip. The dog does seem up-to-date with her inoculations, though."

Neil beamed. "It's good to help dogs," he said, "but it's nice to help people as well."

"I had to tell Sergeant Moorhead, of course," said Bob. "He's coming to take a statement from Kay.

However, he can't promise that he won't be taking it further. Kay has still committed an offense. Until the quarantine rules change, it's still the law."

"She won't be locked up, will she?" asked Emily.

"No. Under the circumstances he doesn't think she will get more than a small fine."

"I know what she did was technically wrong, Dad," said Neil. "But there was a very good reason for it."

"Possibly," said Bob. "We'll have to hope for the best, eh? There is some good news," he added. "The hospital just called. Your mother and Sarah are on their way home."

Neil and Annie took Jimbo back to the rescue center, then he reunited Annie with her mother in the kennel's office. The little girl began to cry again as Kay explained to her that Lou-Lou had to go away for a while. Annie said something in French, and then, "Can we keep Jimbo?"

Kay looked at Neil. "What's this about a dog called Jimbo?" she asked him.

"Jimbo's in our rescue center," Neil explained. "His owner died, so we're trying to find a new home for him."

A thoughtful expression came over Kay's face. "My parents always had a couple of dogs," she said. "When Lucky died, my father didn't get another because his arthritis was so bad. But it's much better since he had the operation. I wonder if he could give Jimbo a home?"

"I don't see why not," Neil said hopefully, turning to his father. "What do you think, Dad?"

"It's something to think about," Bob said. "The thing is, Jimbo might not take to your father too well. He's a bit of a flirt, you see. He seems to prefer very young ladies!"

Annie was still gazing pleadingly at Kay.

"It may well be worth a try," said Bob. "Why don't you bring your father over when he's better and we'll see how it goes?"

"I'll do that," Kay said.

When Mike Turner arrived soon after, Lou-Lou was cowering beside Kay. "I think she knows that a stranger is going to take her away," said Kay.

As Neil watched Kay pick Lou-Lou up and gently carry her to the car, Neil scratched his head. "The quarantine rules seem pretty silly to me," he said. "If the dog's been vaccinated against rabies, what's the point of all the fuss?"

Mike shook his head vigorously. "I see your point, Neil, but you'd understand the caution if you'd ever seen a case of rabies. We can check that this dog's been vaccinated because of the microchip, but other owners aren't always quite so conscientious. Whatever happens to the quarantine laws in the future, we've got to make sure that rabies doesn't come into

the country. If it reached foxes, there could be an epidemic!"

"I think we should keep Lou-Lou on the website," said Neil, seated in front of the office PC as he and Emily waited for Sarah. Neil was updating the King Street Kennels site and deleting their plea for help in locating the missing dog. "Squirt would never forgive us if we took her off it — although I suppose we'll have to tell her the story sometime."

Emily nodded, then jumped up when she heard the Range Rover on their front driveway. They both

raced outside to meet Sarah. She looked pale after
her time in the hospital, but she was thrilled to be
back home again. Everybody received huge hugs in
turn and Sam got the biggest of all.

"It's vegetable lasagna for dinner tonight," Bob
said. "Especially for Sarah."

"Let me say hello to Fudge first," Sarah replied,
running inside to see her hamster.

As Neil turned to follow her he heard the sound of
another car arriving. His face fell when he saw who
it was. It was Sergeant Moorhead. The policeman
looked distinctly unhappy as he got out of his car
and trudged over to him.

"Oh, no!" Neil whispered to Emily. "I think I'm in
trouble now."

Emily noticed the look on the police officer's face
and then turned to run inside. "Sorry, Neil. You're on
your own with this one." Neil could still hear Emily's
giggles as Sergeant Moorhead stopped in front of
him.

"I've been looking for you, Neil Parker," the red-faced
man said sternly.

"Me, sir?" whispered Neil pathetically.

"Yes, you. When I got back from Padsham, where
I'd been looking for a dog that you'd found already, I
discovered that there was another hunt in progress.
Apparently, Mr. Hamley's class at Meadowbank
School went out for a cross-country run earlier this
afternoon. When one of his pupils disappeared, Mr.

Hamley called us and reported the boy missing. By the time I heard about it my constable and a half dozen officers from Padsham were scouring the countryside in search of one Neil Parker."

"Oops!" Neil croaked.

Sergeant Moorhead's face grew even darker. "When I said that I thought I might be able to solve the mystery, Mr. Hamley said something about an extracurricular essay that was suspiciously good as well. Have you got anything to say for yourself, Neil?"

Neil's jaw gaped. This was not what he had expected. He was in trouble and there was nothing he could say that could get him out of it. For the first time in his life, he was completely lost for words.